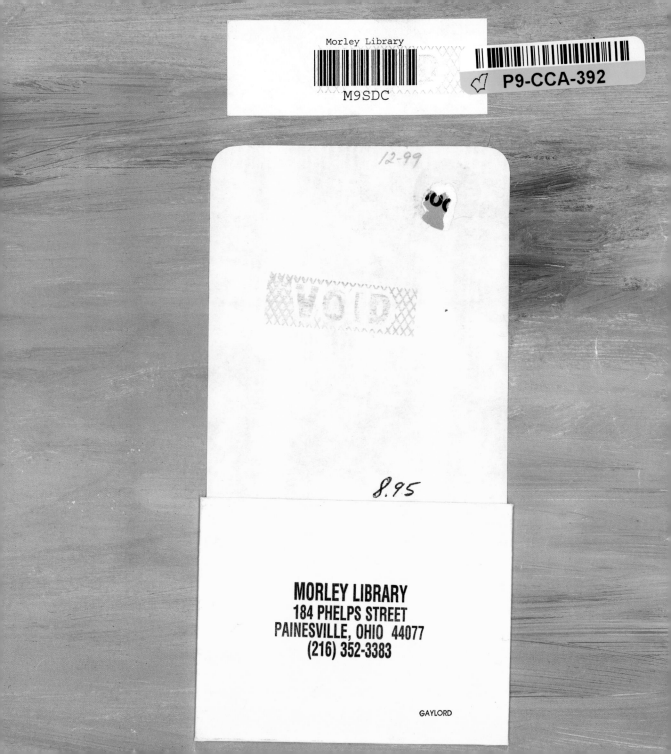

For Ilse, Maya and Soon-Dae

Library of Congress Cataloging-in-Publication Data

Spetter, Jung-Hee, 1969-
   [Koude voeten. English]
   Lily and Trooper's winter / Jung-Hee Spetter. — 1st American ed.
      p.   cm.
   Summary: a little girl and her dog spend the day playing in the snow.
   ISBN 1-886910-39-1 (hardcover)
   [1. Snow—Fiction. 2. Dogs—Fiction.] I. Title.
   PZ7.S7515Liw   1999
      [E]—dc21   98-27970

Copyright © 1998 Lemniscaat b.v. Rotterdam
Originally published in the Netherlands under the title *Koude voeten*
by Lemniscaat b.v. Rotterdam
Printed and bound in Belgium

First American edition

Jung-Hee Spetter

Lily and Trooper's Winter

Front Street 𝟾 Lemniscaat

Asheville, North Carolina

"Good morning, Trooper. Let's go outside and play."

"Look at the snow!"

"Woof!" – "Oh boy, Trooper! A snowman."

"Let's dress him up."

"Wait, Trooper! Don't pull his scarf."

"Whoops!" – "Woof!"

"I think we should go skating now."

"All aboard!"

"Come on, Trooper. We're not moving."

"Ohhhhhhhhhhh!"

"That was exhausting. I'm famished!" – "Woof woof!"

"Now, Trooper, skiing is the best!"

Whoosh!

"Whoops!"

"Moof!"

"I'm finally warm again, Trooper!"

"Mmmmm." – "Rrrrrrrr."

"Trooper! What about the snowman?"

"Mush, Trooper, mush!"

"Okay! One two three, heave! One two three, ho!"

"Uh-oh!" Drip. Drip. Drop.

"Hmmm. That was not a good idea."

"Good night, moon. Good night, snow."

"Good night, Trooper." – "Woof!"